# RAINBOW magic™

This book belongs to

Emily

ISBN: 978-0-545-22175-7

First published in Great Britian by Orchard Books U. K. in 2008.

12 11 10 9 8 7 6 5 4 3 2 1          10 11 12 13 14 15/0
53

New Material Only      Matériaux neufs seulement
Reg. No. 06T-1710609      N° de permis 06T-1710609
Content:      Contenu:
Polyurethane Foam      Mousse de polyuréthane

Printed in China
First Scholastic Printing, May 2010

# My RAINBOW magic™

## Friendship Secrets

Dear Rainbow Magic Friend,

Ever since we met on the ferry to Rainspell Island, we knew we were going to be best friends! This book has space for you to write all about your favorite people — and to learn how to be the best fairy friend ever!

Lots of love,
Kirsty and Rachel xoxo

Based on the books by
**Daisy Meadows**

**Scholastic Inc.**

| New York | Toronto | London | Auckland |
|----------|---------|--------|----------|
| Sydney | Mexico City | New Delhi | Hong Kong |

# A Sprinkling Of Rainbow Magic

On top of being sisters, the Rainbow Fairies are also best friends! It's the little things that make a friendship special, like chatting on the phone and sharing secrets.

## Ruby the Red Fairy

My spell is for smiles
and a thousand kind acts.
Making a friend
is a wonderful pact!

The seven
Rainbow Fairies
have each cast a special
friendship spell for you.
Try reading them out loud
to your best friend!

## Amber the Orange Fairy

My spell is for parties
and meeting to play!
Chatting with friends will
brighten your day.

## Sunny the Yellow Fairy

My spell is for being there
no matter what.
A friend you can count on
is worth a whole lot!

Write down some of the nicest things your best friend has ever done for you, and the things you like most about them.

## Good times and bad...

When Jack Frost didn't get invited to the Midsummer Ball, he caused so much trouble! He took the colors away from Fairyland by banishing the Rainbow Fairies to the human world. Thank goodness Kirsty and Rachel were there to help them — true friends in times of need!

## Heather the Violet Fairy

My spell is for help, splitting problems in two. You never know when your friend may need you!

## Inky the Indigo Fairy

My spell is for giggles, for laughs in the sun. Friendship is priceless, but most of all, fun!

## Sky the Blue Fairy

My spell is for whispers and secrets to share. Open your heart to someone who'll care!

## Fern the Green Fairy

My spell is for trying out daring new things. Do them together, you'll be lifted on wings!

# The Fairy Friendship Promise

How do you become a great best friend?
Every Rainbow Magic fairy makes a special fairy friendship
promise – a pledge to be thoughtful, loyal, and kind. All of the Fun Day Fairies
try their best to remember the promise, even when it means saying they're
sorry or standing up for each other in front of Jack Frost's sneaky goblins!

## R is for...
**Ready for fun.**
A special friendship is
all about sharing jokes
and cheering each
other up!

## A is for...
**Always there.**
Even if you're far away,
a true friend will be
there to chat, listen,
and make you smile.

## I is for...
**In the fairy way.**
Rainbow Magic friends
all believe in fairies.
You never know when
you'll spot one!

## N is for...
**Never angry.**
We all get annoyed
sometimes, but a true
friend never stays
mad for long.

The promise is easy
to remember, because
it spells out the word
RAINBOW. Try to
stick to it every day
of the week!

**B is for...**
**Big-hearted.**
A card in the mail
or a surprise visit proves
what fun it is
to give and to receive!

**O is for...**
**On your side.**
Friends can't agree
all the time, but it's
important to see each
other's point of view.

**W is for...**
**Willing to help.**
Friends shouldn't need
to be asked to help, they
should volunteer! Friends are
always there for each other.

We have both made the fairy
friendship promise. We know
that we can count on each other
through thick and thin!

Kirsty and Rachel xoxo

# My Magical Best Friend

Grace the Glitter Fairy has touched this special page with her shimmery pink wand! She's best friends with Phoebe the Fashion Fairy. This is the place for you to write all about your best friend and some of your favorite memories together!

Name:

The things we do together:

My favorite memories:

What she'll be when she grows up:

Her favorite animal:

The stuff we laugh about:

The Rainbow Magic fairy she most looks like:

Draw a portrait of your best friend in the heart below.

My best friend's signature:

# Say It With Flowers!

When you're a true friend, you are willing to do lots of nice things for someone else. Giving a homemade friendship bracelet or inviting a pal over to watch a DVD will make her feel truly special!

When Kirsty and Rachel helped Ella the Rose Fairy and her friends get the magic petals back from Jack Frost, the Petal Fairies created two beautiful flower garlands for them to wear! Here's how to make a garland for your best friend in whatever colors you like best.

## You will need
- Sheets of crêpe paper in at least two colors
- Scissors
- Needle
- Yarn
- Ruler

1  Fold over your sheets of crêpe paper a few times, and then cut out lots of squares measuring roughly 4 in x 4 in.

2  Pick up one square, and pinch the center with your thumb and forefinger. Gently twist the middle to create a flower shape.

3   Thread the needle with a long piece of yarn and tie a knot in the end. Ask a grown-up to help you push the needle through the twisted part of the paper flower and thread it along the yarn.

4   Twist another crêpe paper square in the same way and thread it onto the yarn. Repeat this lots of times until you have a full string of flowers.

5   When the garland is long enough, tie the ends of the yarn together.

We were so happy with the flower garlands that Ella gave to us!

When we got back from our vacation, the garlands magically transformed into pretty anklets. We always think of our friends, the Petal Fairies, when we wear them.

Kirsty and Rachel xoxo

This beautiful flower chain will also look great hanging in your friend's bedroom!

# Friends Are Fun!

The Dance Fairies use their magic ribbons to get all their friends grooving and enjoying themselves. Call your best friend today and plan some fun activities! Why not pick an activity from this fun-tastic Rainbow Magic list?

## Daytime Disco

You only need one dance partner to put on a rocking disco in your bedroom! Pull the curtains, string up some twinkly lights, and put on some funky music! Wear your sparkliest outfits and try creating your own dance routine or singing along, karaoke-style.

## Garden Giggles

When the sun is out, take the party outside! Lazy afternoons spent threading daisy chains, reading magazines, or sharing a picnic are perfect. Why not organize a game of soccer, build a fort, or ask your parents if you can have a barbecue, too?

## Glittery Arts and Crafts

Fairies love glitter! Ask a grown-up to cover a table with newspapers, gather up some art materials, and have your friends over. Lay out lots of white paper, glue, and tubes of glitter, plus at least three items from the list below:

Gel pens, pictures cut out from old magazines, stick-on gems, ribbons, old wrapping paper, felt-tip pens, balls of yarn, scissors, crayons, scraps of old fabric

## Out and About!

How about an afternoon out with friends? Don't forget to ask a grown-up first! Try ice-skating, the park, shopping, the movies, bowling, or swimming.

## Enchanted Sleepover

Ask your friends to pack their toothbrush, wand, PJs, and favorite Rainbow Magic book – it's time for a fairy sleepover! After dark, turn on night-lights and sit in a fairy circle. Share your favorite storybooks and secrets until the last girl falls asleep!

### Warning:
Getting together causes giggles, and giggles are infectious – once you get started, it's hard to stop!

# My Favorite Fairy Friend

These fairies would love to be your friend! Start at the beginning of the trail and follow the chain of words that you like the most. At the end you'll meet your fairy match!

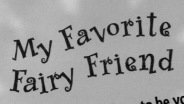

Cupcakes

Playdates

Cherries

START

Songs

Parties

Spells

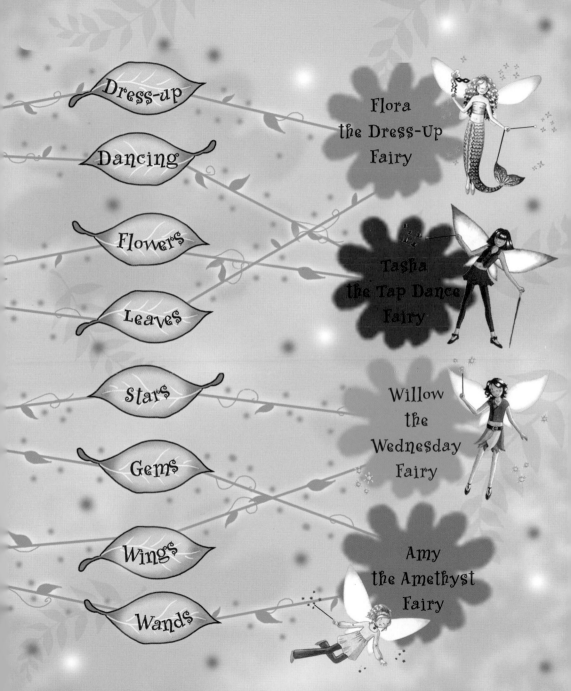

# Magic Across The Miles

Some of our closest friends may live far away. Luckily, the Rainbow Magic fairies and Rachel and Kirsty know all kinds of great ways to keep in touch!

These pretty notes will show your friends that you're thinking about them! Making your own printed stationery is lots of fun, and it's special to receive, too.

## You will need

- Old newspapers
- Cutting board
- Knife
- Potatoes
- Kitchen towels
- Star cookie cutter
- Fork
- Paint
- Saucer
- Blank notepaper and envelopes
- Stickers, glue, and glitter to decorate

1  Cover a table with old newspapers, then ask a grown-up to help you cut a large potato into slices at least 1 inch thick.

2  Lay the slices on kitchen towels and dry them off.

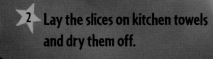

3  Put a potato slice back on the cutting board. Press out a star shape using a cookie cutter, or ask a grown-up to cut one out for you with a knife.

4 Press a fork into the star shape so you can pick it up without touching the potato.

5 Dip the potato into a saucer of bright paint until it is fully coated.

6 Carefully print the star shape in a border around the edge of each sheet of blank notepaper.

7 Use more paint to press a matching star on the back of each envelope.

8 Wait for your starry stationery to dry, then decorate it with stickers and glitter.

## Postcard Pals

Once a month, make a pact with a friend to send each other a postcard. Everybody loves to receive cards, and it's nice to know that you're in someone's thoughts, wherever they may be. You could even have a competition to find out who can find the funniest card each time!

## Instant Messaging

If you both have computers at home, instant messaging is a speedy way of keeping in touch. Ask a grown-up's permission to use the computer, and have them help you set your friend up safely on your online address book or buddy list.

# Show What You Know!

The Weather Fairies have created this quiz to figure out how well you know your best friend! Try to answer as many questions as you can on your own. When you're finished, ask your best friend to mark your answers and total up your scores. You get 1 point for each correct answer!

What does she like for breakfast?

Which clubs does she belong to?

What color are your friend's eyes?

What outfit is she most likely to wear?

What's her favorite pop group?

Where did she last go on vacation?

What's her best subject at school?

What is her favorite color?

What color is her bedroom?

What's the name of her oldest stuffed animal?

What's her favorite food?

What's in her notebook?

Describe her funkiest party outfit!

Which TV show does she like best?

What is her greatest talent?

Name the most surprising thing about her.

Write down her silliest nickname.

Where was her last birthday party?

What sort of books does she read?

Name her favorite hobby.

## 0-6 points
It's a promising start, but there's so much more to discover about your best friend! It's time to do lots more listening to find out all the things that make her tick.

## 7-13 points
Your friend still has a few secrets, but maybe you're still getting to know each other. Keep chatting and sharing and you'll have full points in no time!

## 14-20 points
Great job! You really do know your friend inside out! You take the fairy friendship promise very seriously, and clearly share everything together.

# Furry Friends

Some of the fairies' closest friends are animals – loyal creatures that can always be counted on to play or give a friendly hug.

## Dream Animals!

There are so many animals we can't have as pets, but we can still dream about them. Sit down with a friend and write about the animal you love the most – it might be a whale, tiger, or even a unicorn! Making up stories is a fun way to bring the animal to life, and to share ideas with your friend!

## Sparky!

Georgia's guinea pig, Sparky, is her best friend in the whole world! She can understand every little squeak he makes. It was such a relief when Rachel and Kirsty helped Georgia find him before Jack Frost's naughty goblins could steal him away again!

# My Pet File

Name: ..................................................... Type of animal: ...........................................

Color: .................................................... Favorite food: .............................................

The things my pet likes to play with:

.................................................................................................................................

.................................................................................................................................

The funniest thing my pet has done:

.................................................................................................................................

.................................................................................................................................

Where my pet likes to sleep:

.................................................................................................................................

.................................................................................................................................

Special tricks: ...........................................................................

.................................................................................................................................

Draw a portrait of your real or imaginary pet here:

## Pleased To Meet You!

Kirsty and Rachel have made so many wonderful fairy friend
There's never time to be shy when they meet a new fairy, beca
the girls have magical jobs to do! If you are in a new group, w
not try some ice-breaker games to get you chatting?
You'll be laughing together no time!

At least six players required, plus one fairy godmother.

## The Fairy Name Game

1. Choose one person to be the fairy godmother of the game. Ideally, it should be the girl who knows the most people in the room.

2. Everyone else sits in a circle and thinks up a magical fairy name for themselves. Be as creative as you like – why not use the name of your favorite Rainbow Magic fairy?

3. The players take turns whispering their names to the fairy godmother, who writes them in a list on a sheet of paper.

4. While she is writing, the players should split into two groups and sit opposite each other.

5. When she is ready, the fairy godmother will read out the names once in random order and select a fairy to start the game.

6. The player chooses one of the girls in the other group and tries to guess her fairy name. If she gets it right, the fairy has to come and join her team and she gets another turn. If she guesses wrong, it's the other fairy's turn.

7. Once everyone is on one side, that team is the winner!

# Fairies, Goblins, and Giants

1. This game is played like "rock, paper, scissors," but it has its own funny actions!

2. "Fairies" flutter their arms as if they are flying.

3. "Goblins" make a terrible face and wrinkle their noses.

4. "Giants" stand on tiptoe, and act as tall and as wide as they can.

5. When the game begins, both players act out the part they have chosen: fairy, goblin, or giant. Each character can win against one character and lose against another. However, if you both pick the same character, neither of you scores a point and you must start again.

6. Fairies cast a spell on goblins. Goblins freeze giants. Giants tickle fairies.

7. At the end of each round, the winner is awarded a point. The first player to reach nine points becomes the champion!

Two players required.

Every school vacation, Rainspell Island is packed with visitors. When you see a friendly new face on vacation, use these rules to help start a new friendship:

- Tell them your name
- Ask questions . . .
- and listen to the answers!
- Be honest
- Find some things you both like doing
- Introduce your new friend to your mom or dad

# Step Into the Fairy Ring

Fairy rings are secret, enchanted meeting places where special friends share their thoughts and dreams. Gather in the yard or in your bedroom, then hold hands and share as much Rainbow Magic as you can!

Use this wheel to inspire you to tell your very own fairy tales. Pick a number, read the first line, and then let your imagination carry you away!

1

2 — Amber fluttered up to the dollhouse and knocked on the door . . .

3 — Penny's pony, Glitter, reared up as she saw a sparkling— before her . . .

4 — The bird landed gently in front of Megan. "Can you help me?" she asked . . .

5 — Ella flew back to Fairyland as fast as she could. What was she going to tell Queen Titania?

6 — The goblin banged on Fern's front door. The fairy was running out of places to hide . . .

7 — The Party Fairies could hear a strange whimpering outside. Peering out of the window they saw . . .

"Quick!" said Jenny, grabbing her young fairy friend by the . . .

**Glitter**

**Silver balls**

No one can resist the sparkle of fairy dust! Spoon at least three ingredients from this list into a bowl and then mix them together to make your own fairy dust. When you sit in your fairy ring, sprinkle a pinch of dust into each person's hand to give them extra good luck!

**Sequins**

**Sugar**

**Confetti**

**Flower petals**

Ten ways to make your fairy ring even more magical:

1) Hold hands

2) Wear a twinkly tiara

3) Close your eyes

4) Ask an adult to light a scented candle

5) Whisper gently

6) Speak in rhyme

7) Wear fairy wings

8) Bring your magic wand

9) Light the circle with a flashlight

10) Read fairy poems and spells

# Friends Forever

Congratulations! You really are a true Rainbow Magic friend. All it takes to be a great friend are a few honest words, some kind acts, and lots of patience.

I'd be lost without my best friend Kirsty! We have lots of pictures of each other to make us smile when we're not together. Why not make a best friend picture frame just like mine, then decorate it with pretty stickers?

## You will need

- An empty box with a plastic window
- Pencil
- Ruler
- Scissors
- Glue
- Two photos
- Tape
- Stickers and gift-wrap to decorate

1  Open the box and flatten it. Turn the box over and draw a large rectangle around the see-through window. Make sure there is at least 1 inch between the window and the edge of the rectangle all the way around.

2  Cut out the rectangle and turn the frame shape over.

**3** Put another piece of cardboard from the box behind the frame and trace the outline of the rectangle. Carefully cut this out to create the back of the frame.

**4** Cut out a strip of cardboard 1/2 - inch thick, then use glue to adhere it in the center behind the see-through plastic, dividing the frame in two.

**5** Place the photos in the middle of each window. Ask an adult if you are allowed to trim the photos to fit, if necessary. Use tape to stick them both in place.

**6** Use a little glue to stick the front and back pieces of the frame together.

**7** When your frame is ready, decorate it with pretty stickers and wrapping paper. Make sure that none of the original box can be seen!

# More magical fairy fun!

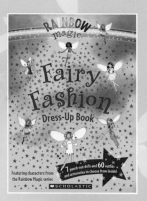

**RAINBOW magic**

Fairy Fashion
Dress-Up Book

Featuring characters from
the Rainbow Magic series

7 punch-out dolls and 60 outfits
and accessories to choose from inside!

SCHOLASTIC

**RAINBOW magic**

Fairy Friends
Sticker Book

Featuring characters from
the Rainbow Magic series

More than 60 full-color
stickers inside!

SCHOLASTIC

**RAINBOW magic**

Fairy Stencils
Sticker Coloring Book

Featuring characters from
the Rainbow Magic series

More than 100 Rainbow Magic
stickers and 16 fairy stencils inside!

SCHOLASTIC

**RAINBOW magic**

Fairy Style
Fashion Sticker Book

More than 150 reusable
Rainbow Magic stickers and
12 cutout dolls inside!

Featuring characters from
the Rainbow Magic...

SCHOLASTIC

Door Hanger Book

**RAINBOW magic**

SCHOLASTIC

**RAINBOW magic**

My
Rainbow
Magic
Birthday
Secrets

Stickers,
horoscopes,
and more
inside!

SCHOLASTIC

**RAINBOW magic**

Friendship
Notes

SCHOLASTIC

Fairy
Friends